THE HAUNTING OF PIP PARKER

A deliciously spooky Christ... ...e by
Flour Babies and *Madame Dou...* e

Anne Fine lives in Edinburgh with her two daughters and various pets. She has written many books for children and young adults. These include *Goggle-eyes*, which won the Carnegie Medal and the Guardian Children's Fiction Award and was successfully dramatized as a BBC TV serial, *Bill's New Frock*, Winner of the Smarties Book Prize, *Flour Babies*, Winner of the Carnegie Medal and the Whitbread Children's Novel Award and *Madame Doubtfire*, which was made into a popular Hollywood feature film.

Emma Chichester Clark won the Mother Goose Award for her first book, *Listen to This*. She has since illustrated a number of children's books including, for Walker, *The Minstrel and the Dragon Pup*, *Good Night, Stella*, and two collections of verse, *Ragged Robin* and *I Never Saw a Purple Cow*. She lives in London.

Some other titles

The Baked Bean Kids
by Ann Pilling / Derek Matthews

Beware Olga!
by Gillian Cross / Arthur Robins

The Finger-eater
by Dick King-Smith / Arthur Robins

Holly and the Skyboard
by Ian Whybrow/ Tony Kenyon

Little Luis and the Bad Bandit
by Ann Jungman / Russell Ayto

Millie Morgan, Pirate
by Margaret Ryan / Caroline Church

A Night to Remember
by Dyan Sheldon / Robert Crowther

Sky Watching
by Dyan Sheldon / Graham Percy

ANNE FINE

THE HAUNTING OF

PIP PARKER

Illustrations by
Emma Chichester Clark

WALKER BOOKS
LONDON

Story first published 1991 in the
Telegraph Magazine as "All I Want for Christmas"

This edition published 1994
by Walker Books Ltd, 87 Vauxhall Walk
London SE11 5HJ

2 4 6 8 10 9 7 5 3 1

Text © 1991 Anne Fine
Illustrations © 1992 Emma Chichester Clark

Printed in England

British Library Cataloguing in Publication Data
A catalogue record for this book
is available from the British Library.

ISBN 0-7445-3093-8

For David Irwin
A.F.

Maybe you're braver than I am.
Maybe it wouldn't spoil your
Christmas Eve to have to lie
awake feeling haunted,
instead of drifting off
to sleep knowing
you'd wake
to find your
stocking
full of
presents.

Maybe you wouldn't mind the night before Christmas being turned into a sort of two-months-late Hallowe'en.

I minded. I minded a lot.

Over there on my desk lay the gifts I'd made…

or saved to buy…

and wrapped up for other people.

Down there at the end
of my bed, across
my feet, lay my big
red (still empty)
Christmas
stocking.

Above my head hung the glittery
Advent calendar I'd made at school,
with only one door left to open.

13

And there, on the far wall,
was what was keeping me
awake – the horrible tiny
golden skull shape that
had been shining at
me off the wall for
a whole week.

Maybe you have stronger nerves than I do. But I couldn't sleep. And I'm not a baby. I managed well enough when I slept over at Great Aunt Belle's, and the branches of her ash tree waved in front of the street light and threw the creepiest shadows you've ever seen over the bedroom wall.

I was fine at Alex's house too,
even if it did take me a bit of time to
work out that those weird snaky
things that kept flitting across the
ceiling were just car headlights
turning into Mappin Road.

But here in my own home I was a
total wreck. I shut my eyes to go to
sleep, and had to keep opening
them again, to see if the
skull was still

watching me. Not that it had eyes,
exactly. It was just a shape on the
wall, a gleaming shape, about the
size of my thumb. But it worried
me. I couldn't take my eyes off it.
And so I couldn't get to sleep, and
all week I'd been going around like
a zombie, too tired even to think.

And they all kept asking me things.

Pips, what was the name of that rather nasty plastic thing you saw in the shop window and liked so much?

It's Granny on the phone. She wants to know if Pip likes poetry. Do you like poetry, Pip?

Simply as a matter of interest, Pip, did you ever find your bike chain?

I'd try to concentrate. After all,
I know as well as you do that it's
important to keep your wits about
you when people are asking you
this sort of question in the last few
days before Christmas. Too many
wrong answers, and you can fetch
up with a pile of junk.

But I was too sleepy to think. And yawning so hard, I couldn't answer anyway.

"Pip! There's only a couple of days left. Please give us a few ideas. What sort of things would you like?"

"Books?"

"Clothes?"

"Pens?"

"Cassettes?"

"Computer stuff?"

Already I was deep in another
yawn.

"Pip!"

I made a real effort. But all I
wanted for Christmas was to stop
being haunted. And that's what
I told them.

"All I want for Christmas is for
someone to get rid of that horrible
thing on my bedroom wall."

"There's nothing on your wall."

"Oh yes, there is!"

"No, there isn't. It's all your imagination. Three times the whole lot of us have trooped upstairs to look for it for you. And every single time there was nothing there."

It came back as soon as you'd gone.

I can't help it. When I get tired, I get scratchy-tempered. That's just the way I am. I need my sleep. And so, all through last week, when they kept asking me, "Have you decided what you want for Christmas yet?", I kept saying over and over (though I knew how it was annoying them):

All I want for Christmas is a *nice blank wall*.

You could hear their voices going all frosty. "Right, then. I suppose it will just have to be a surprise."

No one believed me. Nobody offered to come up and have another look. And I could see their point.

After all, it was true that they'd
been up three times already. Three
evenings in a row, when I came
down in my pyjamas to complain,
they'd all laid their drinks down
with a sigh and trooped up the
stairs, one after another, moaning.

I'll tell you Pip's problem.
Too much television.

It was there, though. Oh, yes. It was there gleaming at me, as it had been all week. I knew I could go down one last time, but they'd probably get ratty, and might even start teasing me again about the snack Granny had insisted on leaving out "for Santa".

Who made these little cake things? Was it Pip?

No, I was better off up in my bedroom, lying awake staring at the wall and wondering just how the horrible gleaming little skull shape knew exactly when to fold up and disappear.

The last person in the family to come up and have a look was my mother. I heard her hurrying up the stairs and along the landing towards my bedroom, not even stopping to admire the new lamp she'd bought so that Granny could get from the spare room to the bathroom without tripping over the frayed patches in the carpet.

Then she burst through my door.

"Where is it, then?"

And, of course, it had vanished.

"It was here just a moment ago. I was watching it. Honestly."

"Oh, Pip!"

"Just stay a few minutes. Keep absolutely quiet, and see if you can fool it into coming back."

Sighing, she leaned back against the door, and waited.

The seconds passed.

Bored and impatient, she started to drum her fingers behind her on the panels of the door.

"Sssh!" I warned.

She was quiet.

A few more seconds passed. Then:

"Pip! I can't stay here all night. Either it's here, or it isn't. And it isn't."

"But it was here. Only a minute ago."

She swung the door open again, and went out.

"I'll shut this behind me," she

said. "So the noise from downstairs doesn't keep you awake."

"I'll be awake anyway," I told her. But she'd already gone.

And she was no more than a few
steps along the landing before I
turned back, and there it was again!
On the wall...
Gleaming at me...

And that's when I did exactly
what you would do. I gave up.
I gave up trying to have a normal
Christmas Eve. I gave up trying
to sleep.

I simply lay in bed and waited.

And waited.

And waited.

And waited and waited and waited.

And that's
how I came to
stay awake longer
than anyone else my
age, ever, on Christmas Eve.
That's how, when I heard the
rustling outside, and the rattle of
my doorknob, I quickly closed my
eyes and pretended as hard as I
could that I was fast asleep.

I'm not daft. And I wanted my
stocking filled.

I have to tell you, if you didn't know, that Santa's not quite as portly as he looks in most of the pictures you see about. It wasn't easy to tell in the dark, but if you

want my opinion he's no fatter
than my father. He's no taller
either. And he uses much the same
    language when he stubs his toe
            against the bedstead.

However, unlike my father, he brought me all I want for Christmas. And this is how.

First, he stepped down to the bottom of my bed. I could hear the rustle of presents being stuffed in my stocking. I thought I'd be safer if I turned my face away. You never know.

I'm sure I'm as good as you are at pretending I'm fast asleep, but you know as well as I do that, once you think someone might be watching you, even in the dark, you get this urge to grin.

So I made a sort of fast-asleep, lip-smacking sound and rolled over restlessly to face the other way.

It was safe to open my eyes now.
And there, on the wall, was the
gleaming little skull shape.

Behind me, the heavy footsteps
went back towards the door.
The skull shape disappeared.

Did I move my foot? I'm sure
I didn't move my foot, but it is
true that, just at that moment, my
Christmas stocking slipped off the
bed on to the floor.

The footsteps came back down
to the bottom of my bed again.

The skull shape reappeared.
I felt a fumbling round my feet.

Then my stocking was laid
down on top of them.

The footsteps went back to the door. The shape on the wall vanished.

I moved my foot – only a tiny bit. I didn't mean to tip the stocking on to the floor again.

I won't tell you what Santa
muttered. You wouldn't want to
know, and, if you did, your family
wouldn't want you
to repeat it.

The footsteps came back down
to the end of the bed.

The skull shape reappeared. The
stocking landed on the bed again.
(Quite hard.)

The footsteps went back to the door. The skull shape vanished.

And suddenly, instantly, in a flash, I had all I wanted for Christmas! And I don't mean a stocking full of presents.

No! I didn't care if what was crushing my feet was wonderful presents I'd longed for all my life, or just some old heap of bike chains and poetry books and winter clothes. (To be perfectly honest with you, even now I haven't bothered to pull them out of the stocking and unwrap them.)

No. All I did was slip out of bed,
pad over to the door in my bare feet,
and stuff that stupid skull-shaped
keyhole so full of torn up scraps of
wrapping paper that no light would
ever again be able to shine through
from the other side and make
gleaming shapes on my wall.

Maybe you're brighter than
I am. Maybe you would have
cottoned on the very
first evening, and
known straight
away that the
new lamp on
the landing
was to blame.

Maybe you would have realized at once that the reason nobody else could ever see the skull shape on the wall was because they were leaning against the door and blocking the light through the keyhole. Maybe.

Well, you may be brighter than I am, but you couldn't be more tired. I'm going off to sleep now – my first good sleep for a week. Oh, I know the whole lot of them will be at me again in the morning.

It won't do them any good. I won't even be awake to hear. They can go ahead and open their presents without me. I have all I want for Christmas already – a nice blank wall. And that means a good, long, deep and dreamless sleep. I'm starting it right now.

And I shan't give my best present up that easily.

Neither would you.